RABBIT STEW

WENDY WAHMAN

BOYDS MILLS PRESS
AN IMPRINT OF HIGHLIGHTS
Honesdale, Pennsylvania

Rusty and Rojo toiled and tilled in their vegetable garden all summer long.

"Plump, yet firm," said Rusty.
"Perfectly so," said Rojo.
At long last, the time is ripe
for our prizewinning . . .

We need lean, green runner beans,

purple leaves of kale,

and crunchy orange carrots,

There's No Place Like Hole

THE HOLE FAMILY

Hole is Where the Heart is

for our splendid

RABBIT STEW.

The hole
Shebang

crisp stalks of celery,

and roly-poly blueberries,

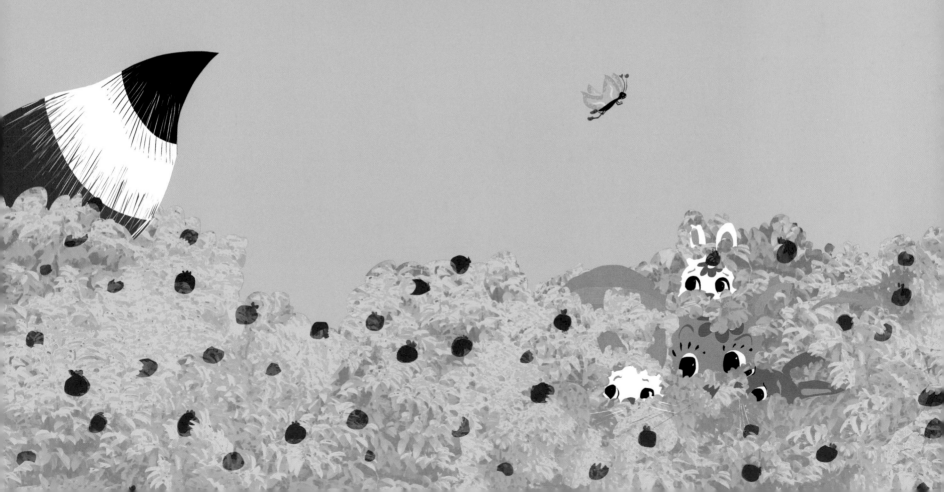

for our marvelous

RABBIT STEW.

We need juicy red tomatoes,

fresh sprigs of parsley,

and sweet yellow peppers,

white . . .

bowl . . .

For my dear husband, Joe.

Boyds Mills Press
An Imprint of Highlights
815 Church Street
Honesdale, Pennsylvania 18431
boydsmillspress.com
Printed in China

ISBN: 978-1-62979-583-6
Library of Congress Control Number: 2016942363

First edition
10 9 8 7 6 5 4 3 2 1

Designed by Anahid Hamparian
Production by Sue Cole
The text of this book is set in Playtime with Hot Toddies and Liquid Embrace.
The illustrations are done in Photoshop using the lasso tool.

for our favorite Rabbit,
Stew —and his family, too!